CW00498864

A Kalmus Classic Edition

Cornelius

GURLITT

BUDS AND BLOSSOMS
TWELVE MELODIOUS STUDIES

Opus 107

FOR PIANO

K 03494

Buds and Blossoms.

Blüthen und Knospen.

Allegretto.

C. GURLITT. Op. 107.

Printed in the U.S.A.

4

Allegretto scherzando.

3.

8

Allegretto grazioso.

4.

14

Moderato grazioso.

7.

20

Allegretto grazioso.

9.

26

Allegretto scherzando.

11.

molto pronunziato.